DEAR MOUSE FRIENDS, WELCOME TO THE

STONE AGE!

WELCOME TO THE STONE AGE . . . AND THE WORLD OF THE CAVEMICE!

CAPITAL: OLD MOUSE CITY

POPULATION: WE'RE NOT SURE. (MATH DOESN'T EXIST YET!) BUT BESIDES CAVEMICE, THERE ARE PLENTY OF DINOSAURS, WAY TOO MANY SABER-TOOTHED TIGERS, AND FEROCIOUS CAVE BEARS — BUT NO MOUSE HAS EVER HAD THE COURAGE TO COUNT THEM!

TYPICAL FOOD: PETRIFIED CHEESE SOUP

NATIONAL HOLIDAY: GREAT ZAP DAY, WHICH CELEBRATES THE DISCOVERY OF FIRE. RODENTS EXCHANGE GRILLED CHEESE SANDWICHES ON THIS HOLIDAY.

NATIONAL DRINK: MAMMOTH MILKSHAKES

CLIMATE: Unpredictable, WITH FREQUENT METEOR SHOWERS

cheese soup

milkshake

MONEY

SEASHELLS OF ALL SHAPES AND SIZES

MEASUREMENT

THE BASIC UNIT OF MEASUREMENT IS BASED ON THE LENGTH OF THE TAIL OF THE LEADER OF THE VILLAGE. A UNIT CAN BE DIVIDED INTO A HALF TAIL OR QUARTER TAIL. THE LEADER IS ALWAYS READY TO PRESENT HIS TAIL WHEN THERE IS A DISPUTE.

Geronimo

Trap

Thea

Benjamin

Hercule Poirat

Grandma R

Geronimo Stilton

CAVEMICE

SURFING FOR SECRETS

Scholastic Inc.

Published by Scholastic Inc., 557 Broadway, New York, NY 10012. SCHOLASTIC and associated logos are trademarks and/or registered trademarks of Scholastic Inc.

Stilton is the name of a famous English cheese. It is a registered trademark of the Stilton Cheese Makers' Association. For more information, go to www.stiltoncheese.com.

This book is a work of fiction. Names, characters, places, and incidents are either the product of the author's imagination or are used fictitiously, and any resemblance to actual persons, living or dead, business establishments, events, or locales is entirely coincidental.

ISBN 978-0-545-74617-5

Text by Geronimo Stilton
Original title *Mordosauri in mare . . . tesoro da salvare!*
Cover by Flavio Ferron
Illustrations by Giuseppe Facciotto (design) and Alessandro Costa (color)
Graphics by Marta Lorini

Special thanks to Tracey West
Translated by Julia Heim
Interior design by Becky James

12 11 10 9 8 7 6 5   20 21/0

Printed in the U.S.A.   40
First printing 2015

MANY AGES AGO, ON PREHISTORIC MOUSE ISLAND, THERE WAS A VILLAGE CALLED OLD MOUSE CITY. IT WAS INHABITED BY BRAVE *RODENT SAPIENS* KNOWN AS THE CAVEMICE.

DANGERS SURROUNDED THE MICE AT EVERY TURN: EARTHQUAKES, METEOR SHOWERS, FEROCIOUS DINOSAURS, AND FIERCE GANGS OF SABER-TOOTHED TIGERS. BUT THE BRAVE CAVEMICE FACED IT ALL WITH A SENSE OF HUMOR, AND WERE ALWAYS READY TO LEND A HAND TO OTHERS.

HOW DO I KNOW THIS? I DISCOVERED AN ANCIENT BOOK WRITTEN BY MY ANCESTOR, GERONIMO STILTONOOT! HE CARVED HIS STORIES INTO STONE TABLETS AND ILLUSTRATED THEM WITH HIS ETCHINGS.

I AM PROUD TO SHARE THESE STONE AGE STORIES WITH YOU. THE EXCITING ADVENTURES OF THE CAVEMICE WILL MAKE YOUR FUR STAND ON END, AND THE JOKES WILL TICKLE YOUR WHISKERS! HAPPY READING!

Geronimo Stilton

WARNING! DON'T IMITATE THE CAVEMICE. WE'RE NOT IN THE STONE AGE ANYMORE!

WAKE UP, GRANDSON!

It was EARLY morning — really, really early. And I was really, really **snoring**, tucked under my mammoth fur blanket in my cave in *Old Mouse City* when suddenly . . .

Oh, excuse me, I haven't introduced myself. My name is Stiltonoot, **GERONIMO STILTONOOT**, and I am the editor of *The Stone Gazette*.

The Stone Gazette is

2

the most famouse newspaper in prehistory. (It's also the only one!) Anyway, I was snoring louder than a **ROARING** T. rex when suddenly I heard a loud call.

"ROCK-A-DOODLE-DOOOOOO!"

I **JOLTED** awake. The sound of my cave rooster had roused me from my sleep by its crow!

I had just closed my eyes and put my **pillow** over my head when I heard a thundering voice.

"**WAKE UP**, Grandson! This is no time for snoring!"

CAVE ROOSTER
This alarm helps me get up on time!

3

"WH♀? WHaT? WHeRe?"

I yelled, jolting awake again.

The voice kept thundering. "Wake up! The sun is high in the sky, the pterodactyls are flapping around the forest, the villagers are busy working, and here you are, snoring under your covers like a MaMMotH with a cold!

"Look at you!" the voice went on. "You're as PALE as provolone. Your measly muscles look like strings of mozzarella. You need to get up and get some EXERCISE!"

Now, I am a patient mouse — but this abuse was just too much. I lifted my pillow to confront the rodent who had woken me, and then I understood.

It was my GRANDMA RATROCK! She is one strict mouse, all right. She is so FIERCE she could make an angry T. rex turn tail and run.

"But, Grandma," I protested. "I have the right to rest a little bit. I work very hard at the newspaper."

"Rest? You're a Stiltonoot. Stiltonoots don't need rest!" Grandma Ratrock scolded me. "Now get out of that bed and follow us!"

I scratched my head. "What do you mean 'FOLLOW US'? I only see one of you."

That's when I heard another voice.

"Good morning, Uncle Geronimo!"

That was my beloved nephew Benjamin.

"Rise and shine, big brother. It's time to go!"

And that was my sister, Thea.

Well, I couldn't say no to my entire family!

"Bones and stones!" I muttered as they pushed me out of my cave before I could even eat breakfast.

Move it!

??? But...

But where was I going? I didn't even know!

"Pick up the

pace, Geronimo," my sister urged. "We need to get to the port **right away!**"

A strong gust of wind hit us as we rushed to the port. The hot and rushing wind marks the beginning of summer in Old Mouse City.

WHOOOOOOOOOSH!

"Can somebody please tell me why we are going to the port?" I asked, exasperated.

"We are going to see **LEO EDISTONE'S** new invention!" Benjamin answered.

"Yes, he calls it a **Wavebreaker Board**," my sister, Thea, added.

Wavebreaker Board? That sounded dangerous to me. In fact, it sounded like a **sea** of trouble was in store.

Oh, how right I was!

AAAAAARGH!

A crowd of rodents had gathered at the **PORT**, waiting to see Leo Edistone and his new invention. The gusty wind churned the high waves, and the hot air caused them to swirl spectacularly and then CRASH on the dock.

My cousin Trap had prepared two platforms on the dock in front of the Rotten Tooth Tavern so the citizens of Old Mouse City could attend the show — and binge on tasty treats from his restaurant.

With a very **serious** look on his snout, Leo Edistone walked up to one of the platforms.

"Fellow citizens of Old Mouse City!" Leo began. "My new invention is even more genius than sliced cheese! I spent days and nights in my cave, performing HUNDREDS of calculations, making THOUSANDS of notes, and stringing together MILLIONS of brilliant thoughts . . ."

"Thea," I whispered to my sister. "He is the most boring rodent in prehistory!"

Then Leo held up a WOODEN board. It didn't look like anything special.

"Behold my

My latest genius invention!

Wavebreaker Board!" Leo said. "With this board, you can ride the waves like an agile dolphinosaurus!"

"OOOOOOOOOOOOOOH!" murmured the crowd.

"Now, I just need one very courageous, very agile, and very SPORTY rodent to step forward," Leo continued. "Who will volunteer?"

Everyone immediately took a step BACKWARD — except for me, because I was too tired and just not FAST enough. So it looked like I had stepped forward!

Leo grabbed me by the paw. "Well done! We have a brave VOLUNTEER!"

"Um, there's been a mistake," I tried to explain. "I am not very sporty. Or agile. Or courageous."

"Nonsense!" yelled Grandma Ratrock.

My grandmother pushed through the crowd. "Geronimo is very **SPORTY**! He takes after his grandmother!" she bragged.

Leo *SHOVED* the board into my paws. "Great! You're ready to go!"

Then he *PUSHED* me off the rocks and right into the ocean.

That's when I realized Leo hadn't explained how his board worked!

"**Heeelp!**" I yelled as a wave crashed into me.

I would never survive these wild, swirling waters.

PETRIFIED CHEESE, I WAS TOO YOUNG TO GO EXTINCT!

I panicked, kicking and splashing in the churning water.

"**HEEEEEEEELP!**" I yelled again.

Then I saw it, way out on the horizon — a **GIGANTIC** wave as tall as a T. rex was speeding toward the shore!

"Hold on to the board with both paws!" Leo yelled.

I gripped the board tightly. Instinctively, I began to kick behind me. The board was keeping me AFLOAT.

"Now climb on it!" Leo called out.

"Climb on it?" That sounded **DANGEROUS**. But the giant wave was getting closer, so I did it. Somehow, I managed to keep my balance.

"Way to go, Uncle Ger!" Benjamin cheered.

I turned my head and waved at Benjamin. I was doing it!

"CAREFUL!" Thea called out.

"Why do I need to be careful?" I yelled back. "I'm doing great!"

When I turned my head, I suddenly understood. I was about to **crash** into a giant rock!

OW! OW! OW! THAT REALLY HURT!

AAAARGH!

Leo tossed a ROPE into the ocean with a hook on the end. The hook latched onto my clothes, and he PULLED me back to shore.

"Wonderful!" said Leo, turning to the crowd. "As you can see, my Wavebreaker Board is very easy to use!"

"What? You must mean that it's VERY DANGEROUS!" I corrected him.

Suddenly, Leo cried out in alarm . . .

Aaah!

A MOUSE LOST AT SEA!

"Look! There is a **mouse lost at sea**!" Leo cried, pointing.

We all followed his gaze and . . .

FLAMING FIREBALLS!

A rodent was stranded way out in the water, **thrashing** his arms about.

A mouse lost at sea!

He desperately tried to stay afloat among the **waves**.

There was no time to lose! We had to **HELP** him! Grandma Ratrock hopped off the dock and into a boat.

"**JUMP IN!**" she yelled to me, Benjamin, and Thea.

"I'll take the oars," Grandma Ratrock said. "Thea, stay with me. Geronimo and Benjamin, go to the stern of the boat to keep us **BALANCED**!"

MOUSE LOST AT SEA!

Heeeeeeeeeelp!

The wind whipped around us as we got into place. Grandma began to row, and in the wink of a whisker, we were in the middle of the choppy sea on that small boat.

The citizens of Old Mouse City looked at us from the stands, anxiously holding their breath. Would we reach the rodent in time?

Luckily, Grandma Ratrock has very **STRONG** arms. We reached that rodent in a flash! Thea leaned out of the boat and extended a paw toward him.

"Give me your paw!" Thea yelled over the waves. "I'll pull you up!"

With Thea's help, the castaway climbed into the boat, finally safe from the waves. Our **MISSION** was complete!

When we returned to the shore, our fellow citizens cheered.

"Hooray for the Stiltonoots!"

Then I heard a very pleasant call from the stands.

"You were wonderful, Geronimo!"

Bouncing boulders, it was Clarissa, the daughter of the village shaman, Bluster Conjurat. I happen to think that Clarissa is the most fascinating rodent in the whole PREHISTORIC world! In fact, I am crushing on her like a prehistoric rock!

"Um, thanks . . . I mean, really . . . well, I mean . . . do you really think that I was wonderful?" I asked her.

She blew me a kiss from the stands. I blushed so hard that my fur turned pink!

19

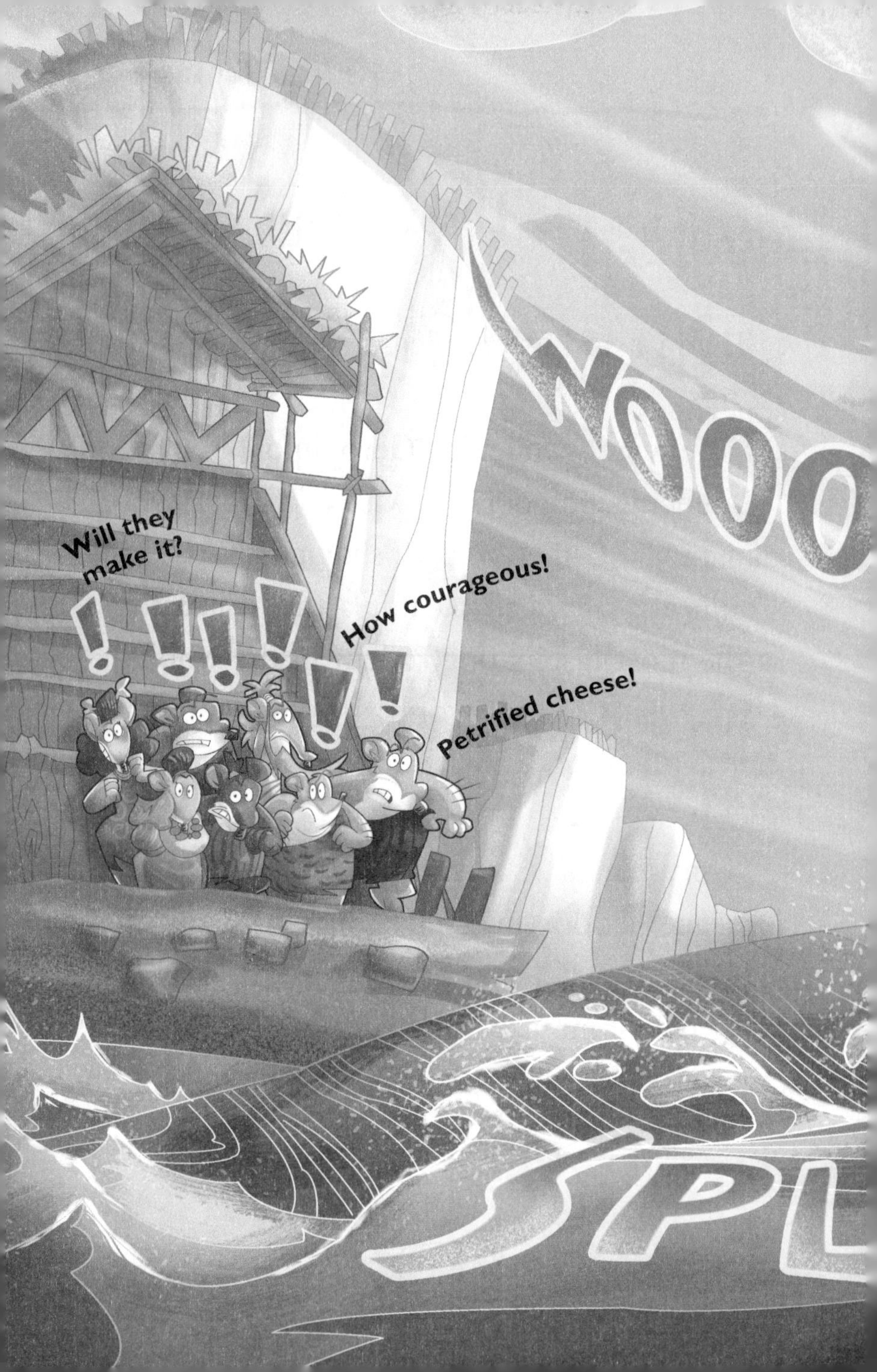
Will they make it?
How courageous!
Petrified cheese!
WOOO
SPL

MY NAME IS BART BARNACLE!

"Th-thank you," I stammered. But then Clarissa — and everyone else in the stands — gathered around the rodent who we had RESCUED. He was standing on the dock, wrapped in a FUR blanket.

I was able to get a better look at him. He had honey-colored fur and dark black hair that he wore tied up on top of his head. I had never seen a hairstyle like that in Old Mouse City before!

He was dressed rather strangely, too. For one thing, his clothing had a skull pattern on it.

I also noticed something hanging around

his neck. A stone key dangled from a leather cord.

The strange rodent sighed and began to tell his story in a sad voice.

"My name is Bart Barnacle, and I am a pirate," he said. "I come from far away. Very, very, very, very far away."

"Yes, we get that," I said a little impatiently.

"I come from the Land of the Rising Sun, from Black Rock Island," Bart went on. "I was so happy down there!"

Bart sighed again, missing his **home**.

BART BARNACLE

NAME: BART BARNACLE

HOME: BLACK ROCK ISLAND, FOUNDED BY THE PREHISTORIC PIRATE DYNASTY

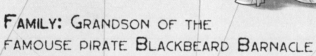

FAMILY: GRANDSON OF THE FAMOUSE PIRATE BLACKBEARD BARNACLE

PROFESSION: PREHISTORIC PIRATE

SPECIALTY: EXPLORER

DISTINGUISHING MARKS: A DARK BLACK TAIL

FAVORITE THING: HE NEVER PARTS WITH THE MYSTERIOUS STONE KEY THAT HIS PIRATE GRANDFATHER GAVE HIM.

HIS SECRET: THAT KEY UNLOCKS A MYSTERIOUS TREASURE!

"I loved growing up there, raised by my grandfather, the famouse pirate **BLACKBEARD BARNACLE**. And I had so many friends!" Bart went on. "But one day, my happiness ended. The other pirates made me an official explorer. I set sail on my boat to travel the **DANGEROUS** southern seas.

"While I was traveling, a huge **crocosaurus** rammed into my boat! The boat capsized, and I was **thrown**

off the deck and into the water! I grabbed on to a wooden trunk and FLOATED for days and days until you found me," Bart explained with a sniffle. "Now you know how I ended up here.

"So here I am," Bart continued. "Far from home in a strange land. With no friends or family. All I have is this key."

"How sad!" said Thea.

I felt sorry for this lost rodent, but I

was Curious, too.

"So, what is that key for?" I asked.

Bart touched it with his paw. "My grandfather, Blackbeard Barnacle, gave this key to me when I left," he said. "It is a legendary key that has been handed down through generations of pirates."

"And what does it open?" I asked, impatient again.

"Why, the Lost Treasure of the Prehistoric Pirates, of course!" Bart replied, and everyone gasped.

THE MYSTERY OF THE LOST TREASURE

Everyone started talking at once. A **lost treasure**? Where was it? *What* was it? Pirate gold? Crates of aged cheddar?

Then **Bluster Conjurat** hit his cane on the ground.

"**LISTEN!**" he said, and everyone stopped talking. "The treasure that Bart Barnacle seeks truly exists. And it is here, on our island!"

"How do you know that for sure, you **old donut**?" asked Grandma Ratrock, who didn't believe anyone, ever. "We never even heard of the Lost Treasure of the Prehistoric Pirates before today."

"Because I am the shaman of this village," Bluster snapped, "and mysteries are my job, cheese breath!"

Grandma Ratrock waved her **CLUB** under his snout. "Who are you calling 'cheese breath'?" she asked **ANGRILY.**

I stepped between them. "Let's all stay

calm, please, and hear what Bluster has to say," I said. "**Everyone** on this island has the right to express their opinion freely."

Bluster nodded at me. "Thank you, Stiltonoot," he said.

Then he placed a **PAW** on the pirate's shoulder. "Bart Barnacle, if it is true that you belong to the dynasty of **prehistoric pirates**, then I believe that the **key** around your neck really is the **key** to the lost treasure. And I know just where to find it!"

"Then **please** tell me where it is, shaman!" Bart begged.

Bluster smiled. (He loves being the **center of attention**.)

Then he cleared his throat

Tell me!

30

and said, "Listen, citizens of Old Mouse City! In case you forgot, I, Shaman Bluster Conjurat, am the only one who knows the SECRETS of the Cave of Memories!"

Everyone started to whisper.

"Yes, he is the shaman. He should know."

Bluster continued. "On the walls of the Cave of Memories, there are cave PAINTINGS! One of them tells the story of the Lost Treasure of the Prehistoric Pirates!"

Listen to me!

"Hooray for the lost treasure!" cheered the rodents in the crowd.

Then everyone started muttering

again about what the treasure could be.

"Is it a collection of **attack clubs**?" asked Grandma Ratrock.

"Maybe it is the egg of a lost species of racing autosauruses," suggested Thea.

Bluster's eyes shone as he considered the possibilities. "It could be the secret to defeating the saber-toothed tigers," he said hopefully.

"Let's go look for it!" yelled Trap. "Whatever it is, it's **OURS** now!"

Grandma Ratrock NUDGED him. "Grandson, you should be ashamed of yourself. Didn't I teach you any manners? This is not our treasure. It belongs to the **prehistoric pirates**, and I will not allow you to steal it from them!"

"Sorry, Grandma," Trap said. "You know how much I love TREASURES."

"Yes, I do," said Grandma Ratrock. "You can be very greedy, Trap."

Grandma Ratrock turned to Bluster. "I propose that we form an EXPEDITION to find the treasure! It shall be me, Thea, Benjamin, you, Bart Barnacle, and Geronimo. He may be a fool, but he is not greedy."

I wasn't sure if that was a compliment, but I was glad to be included. My whiskers started to tremble with excitement.

We were about to go on a journey with a real Pirate to find a real treasure. This had all the makings of . . .

A MOUSERIFIC ADVENTURE!

ATTACK OF THE TIGERS

But we had all forgotten a very small, very tiny, very minuscule detail.

"Moldy mozzarella!" Bluster jumped up and smacked his paw against his forehead. "How could we forget? Our city is currently under siege by the saber-toothed tigers! Trumpeting triceratops, this is bad!"

Unfortunately, the shaman was right. It happened every year at the start of summer. Led by the FEROCIOUS Tiger Khan, the stinky Saber-Toothed Squad surrounded our village. They camped on the outskirts, hoping to stuff themselves with rodents.

They were *sneaky*. They hid behind rocks along the roadside, waiting to **GrAB** any poor, unsuspecting rodent who passed by. Then they would roast him up with prehistoric potatoes on the side!

Things were starting to look **bad** for our adventure. The road to get to the Cave

Chomp!

Growl!

Growl!

of Memories was FULL of tigers. What could we do?

But Grandma Ratrock wasn't worried. "Calm down, you silly shaman," she told Bluster. "I know a shortcut that leads right to the Cave of Memories. We just have to pass through the Hey Hey Forest."

"But the Hey Hey Forest is home to the musky baboons, allies of the saber-toothed tigers!" I pointed out.

BONES AND STONES, HOW SCARY!

"I'm not afraid of any baboons," Grandma said. "Come on! Let's get this show on the road."

We couldn't argue with Grandma Ratrock. The six of us headed into the Hey Hey Forest as quietly as mice (because that's what we are), hoping the baboons wouldn't notice us.

At first, things went **smoothly** as we made our way through the trees. Then I stepped in something SQUISHY.

I looked down at my foot—and it was **BLUe**! I had stepped in some beany pterodactyl dung! The stinky smell made me sneeze.

"ACHOO!"

"Geronimo, *shhh!*" warned Thea.

BLUE PTERODACTYL DUNG

The blue dung of the beany pterodactyl is the stinkiest poo of the Stone Age. It is probably due to the all-bean diet of the pterodactyls.

Warning: If this blue dung falls on you, it will stain your fur!

But it was too late. A storm of **coconuts** came flying at us!

BONK BONK BONK

"Take cover!" Thea yelled. "The baboons are **attacking**!"

The musky baboons were everywhere — up in the palm trees, hanging from **vines**, and hiding in the bushes. And every single one of them was **bombarding** us with coconuts!

The baboon who appeared to be their leader seemed to have it in for me. He kept hurling **coconuts** at me until a huge bump grew on my head!

WHAT A PALEOLITHIC PAIN!

There was nowhere to take shelter from that coconut storm.

The situation was **hopeless**. There was no way out. We were in **big trouble**!

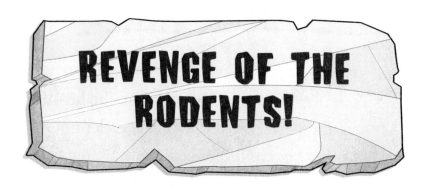

REVENGE OF THE RODENTS!

It looked like we might have to turn back. The baboons would not stop **BONKING** us with coconuts!

Then I saw Grandma Ratrock whispering into Thea's ear. Thea grinned.

"Excellent idea, Grandma!" Thea said.

They picked up their **CLUBS** and started **SWINGING** at the coconuts. They batted the coconuts right back at the baboons!

The coconuts hit the baboons on the head! It was the perfect revenge of the rodents!

Another coconut WHIZZED toward Thea, and she whacked it with her club.

WHOOOSH!

It soared back into the trees.

Benjamin, Bart Barnacle, Bluster, and I picked up our clubs, too. We began to bat away the coconuts. The baboons fell like BOWLING PINS, one by one. We wowed them with our strength and skill!

(Well, most of us wowed them with our strength and skill. I have never been a very SPORTY rodent. But I did my best!)

We kept **BONKING** (or in my case, trying to bonk) the baboons with coconuts until they all ran away. Grandma Ratrock shook her club *triumphantly*.

"We have **WON** the battle!" she cried.

WHAT IS THE PASSWORD?

I had a **BUMP** on my noggin the size of a small **cheese ball**, but otherwise, we were all safe. We left the forest and arrived at the Cave of Memories. At the entrance, we found the cave's rodent guardian and Fluffy, the always-hungry cave bear.

Bluster BRAVELY stepped forward. "You must let us pass!"

"No way, Cheeseheads!" the guardian said. "Who do you think you are? Nobody gets into the Cave of Memories unless they know the PASSWORD!"

At that point, I LIT UP.

"Hey, everybody, this is our lucky day," I said. "I know the password because I've been here before!"*

The guardian raised an eyebrow.

"Oh, you know the PASSWORD, do you?" he asked.

"Yes," I said confidently.

* Read all about it in my adventure *Watch Your Tail!*

"Well, it better be the right one," warned the guardian. "Or I will make sure Fluffy GOBBLES YOU UP, down to the last whisker!"

Fluffy licked his lips and growled.

GRRRRRRRRRRR!

I got the chills.

WHAT SCARY EYES! WHAT SCARY FANGS! WHAT SCARY JAWS!

Petrified cheese! Why did the guardian of the cave have to have a hungry bear for a pet?

GRANDMA RATROCK prodded me. "What is the password, Geronimo?"

"Yes, what is it, Uncle?" asked Benjamin.

"Um, well," I stammered. "It's on the tip of my tongue . . ."

"Geronimo Stiltonoot!" Bluster blurted

out impatiently. "Out with the password!"

Everyone's **EYES** were on me. I turned as **red** as a prehistoric pepper.

HOLEY BOULDERS, I HAD FORGOTTEN THE PASSWORD!

What is it?

Out with it!

Come on, Grandson!

"Let's see here," I muttered, trying to remember. "Open, Sesame? Or maybe . . . Abracadabra? . . . Or mirror, mirror, on the wall?"

Fluffy kept GLARING at me, making me nervous. I couldn't take it anymore.

"I give up! I've got nothing!" I yelled.

And that's when I remembered the password.

"Wait, I know it!" I cried. "The password is 'nothing.'"

That was definitely the password — I had guessed it accidentally the last time I was here!

But the guardian shook his head. "Nope! That's the old password."

"What do you mean?" I protested.

"I mean that for security reasons, the

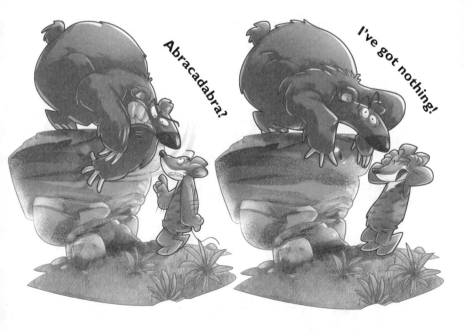

Abracadabra?

I've got nothing!

PASSWORD changes every day," the guardian replied.

I turned as PALE as mozzarella. Now I was really in trouble!

Fluffy growled again, and drool DRIPPED from his hungry jaws as he eyed me.

I turned to my friends and family. "I guess I am headed for extinction," I said fearfully. "I will miss you all. Good-bye!"

As soon as I said that word, the guardian smiled. "Congratulations! Today's password is 'good-bye'!"

FOSSILIZED FETA, I COULDN'T BELIEVE IT! WHAT MEGALITHIC LUCK!

"WELL DONE, GRANDSON!"

Grandma Ratrock said, patting me hard on the back.

"Thanks," I said.

"Every once in a while, you get it right," she added.

Benjamin and Bart Barnacle **hugged** me. Then we entered the Cave of Memories in search of the Lost Treasure of the Prehistoric Pirates!

Thanks!

Hooray!

Good job, Uncle Ger!

THE CAVE OF MEMORIES

Bluster used his ancient **shaman's map** to guide us through the many chambers of the Cave of Memories. Grandma Ratrock and Thea lit **TORCHES** so we could see in the gloomy darkness.

After we passed through Fluffy's Den, we entered the Room of Cave Paintings. The whole history of Old Mouse City was *illustrated* on the walls!

The next room we came to was a **strange** cave filled with **strange** light that gave me the **strange** feeling that a thousand little eyes were spying on me. Then I looked up.

A thousand little eyes really *were* spying on me! We were in the **BAT ROOM**! Thousands of SPARKLY BATS stared at us as they hung upside down from the ceiling, ready to swoop down on us!

Bluster produced a leather sack and took out a pinch of glittery dust. Then he tossed it into the air and sang out:

SPARKLY BATS

Their eyes are so sparkly that they light up their cave just like daylight! These bats never sleep, so their eyes are always open and no one can pass through. But a pinch of powdered cave crystal thrown in the air will put them to sleep.

♪ ♪ "Sparkly bats, ♪ please go to sleep while we sneak by without a peep!" ♪

♪

MAP OF THE CAVE OF MEMORIES

ROOM OF CAVE PAINTINGS

1. Entrance
2. Fluffy's Den
3. Room of Cave Paintings
4. Bat Room
5. Tunnel of the Fanged Spiders
6. Werescorpions' Abyss
7. Underground Labyrinth
8. Lost Treasure of the Prehistoric Pirates
9. Secret Passageway
10. Cemetery (for those trapped in the cave)
11. Guardian's Quarters
12. Piranha Pool

 Mystery Places

The Cave of Memories is the most mysterious place in Old Mouse City. There are countless hallways, chambers, caves, tunnels, and secret passages. It's easy to get lost if you don't have a good guide. The only rodent who knows the cave well is Bluster Conjurat, who inherited the map from his ancestors. However, the cave still holds many secrets that not even Bluster knows about . . .

SPARKLY BATS

FANGED SPIDERS

WERESCORPIONS

The bats quickly **Fell asleep**, and we all breathed a sigh of relief.

"Don't worry," Bluster said. "Not only did my ancestors leave me this map, they left me many **TRICKS** for getting through the cave without losing any fur!"

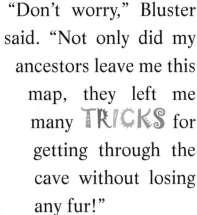

We quietly passed through the Bat Room and found ourselves in the **TUNNEL OF THE FANGED SPIDERS**! I could hear the rustling of thousands of **HAIRY** spider

FANGED SPIDERS

The favorite food of these spiders is the pollen of the very rare swamp rose. Those who enter the Cave of Memories must bring some with them — or risk getting bitten!

legs scampering around us.

Then the rustling came closer.

"Great rocky boulders!" I whispered loudly. "They're going to bite us with their FRIGHTENING fangs!"

But before the spiders got close enough to munch on us, Bluster began to sing.

"All of you spiders,
come get a treat!
It's swamp rose pollen,
and it's very sweet!
So come and get it!
Move those eight feet!"

He produced another pouch and sprinkled PINK POLLEN on the floor of the cave. The spiders stampeded toward it.

We scurried past them. Whew! We were safe once again.

Following his **map**, Bluster led us down a dark and narrow path. Suddenly, he stopped.

"Don't move!" he warned. We had come to the edge of a cliff. "It's the **WERESCORPIONS' ABYSS**!"

The vibration of our pawsteps had already disturbed them. In a flash, a sea of werescorpions emerged from the **DEPTHS** of the abyss!

SQUEAK! WHAT A NIGHTMARE!

WERESCORPIONS

Werescorpions are the most dangerous scorpions of the Stone Age. They can smell a victim a thousand tails away! They are very sensitive to vibrations, and that's how they find their prey. They attack in groups and eat prey down to the bone.

The werescorpions crawled all over us, covering us from the tips of our tails to the tips of our whiskers!

TERRIFIED, I stuttered, "B-B-Bluster, w-what do we do?"

"Don't worry, Stiltonoot, I've got more TRICKS in my fur," he said. Then he produced another pouch and pulled out a rattle. He shook it and sang out:

"Rattle, rattle, rattle, shake, shake, shake!
Werescorpions — give us a break!
Rattle, rattle, rattle, clack, clack, clack!
Go away and never come back!"

The werescorpions didn't like the vibrations of the rattle at all.

"It's working!" Benjamin cried.

The werescorpions **scrambled** off us and back down into the abyss. Whew! We were safe again.

"Thank you, Bluster! You saved our **FUR**," said Benjamin as we safely walked around the abyss.

"You are **amazing**!" Thea told him.

Bart Barnacle didn't say anything, but his eyes were full of **grateful** tears.

Even Grandma was **impressed**. "Bluster,

Now what?

Huh?

I always thought you just liked to brag, but you've really got some skills!"

"She's got that right," I agreed.

"Well, I am a shaman. What did you expect?" Bluster asked.

Then we came to the Underground Labyrinth. Arrows painted on the walls pointed in all different directions.

"You are our guide," I told Bluster. "Which way do we go?" ? ? ?

Hmm ...

Where are we?

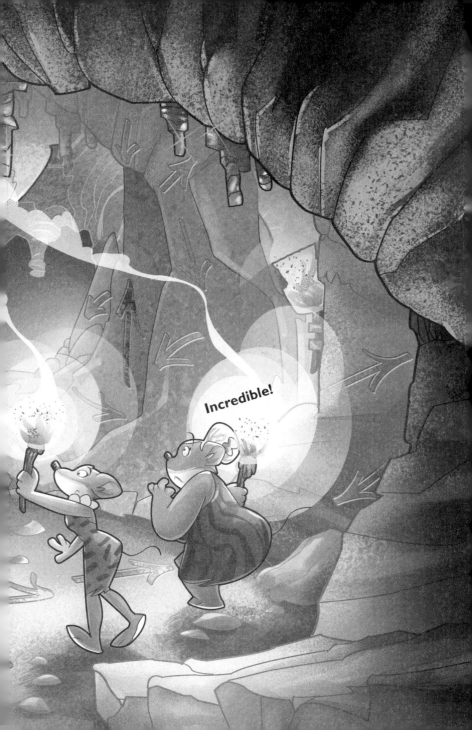

Um . . .

Well . . .

I . . .

I lost the map!

Bluster started **digging** in his pockets. He looked in all his **POUCHES**. He searched his **BEARD**, and he even checked his **UNDERWEAR**!

Then he turned very, very **PALE**. "Um, I have to tell you something," he said nervously. "I, um — I think I, um, lost the map of the Cave of Memories. Basically, um . . . **we're lost!**"

Grandma Ratrock was **FURIOUS**.

"Forget those nice things I said before!" she fumed at Bluster. "You are not a skilled shaman. The only skill you have is messing things up. **YOUR HEAD MUST BE FULL OF ROCKS!**"

THE MYSTERIOUS KEY

We sat on the ground, feeling helpless. Without the map, we had no idea where to go next.

Bart Barnacle **sobbed**. "The Lost Treasure of the Prehistoric Pirates will remain lost forever! Nobody will ever find it now!"

Then I felt Benjamin tug on my fur. "Uncle Ger! I have to tell you something!"

"Not now, Benjamin," I replied. "This is no time to chat."

"But, Uncle, it's very **IMPORTANT**!" Benjamin insisted.

"Benjamin, please try to understand. We

are dealing with something that is more **IMPORTANT** right now," I said. "We are lost. Can't you **SEE** that?"

My nephew shook his head. "No, Uncle, you're the one who doesn't **SEE**. There is a sign on the wall. We aren't lost. We're **EXACTLY** where we need to be!"

We aren't lost!

Only then did I see that Benjamin was pointing to a small **CRACK** in the rock, hidden by the shadows. It wasn't an ordinary crack — it was in the shape of a **keyhole**!

"Come see what Benjamin has found," I said, and everyone got up to examine the crack in the **STONE** wall.

Bluster didn't like to see a young rodent show him up.

"These walls are thousands of years old," he said. "It's normal for them to have CRACKS. This is nothing special."

Thea examined it closely. "Benjamin is right!" she announced. "There is something strange about the shape of this crack. It looks like a keyhole. In fact, I bet you a hundred shells that the stone key that Bart Barnacle wears around his neck fits this crack!"

How strange . . .

Hmm . . .

Bart Barnacle approached the wall. "There's only one way to find out," he said. "I've got to try this key!"

The pirate removed the key from around

his neck and slipped it into the hole.

FOSSILIZED FETA! It not only fit perfectly, but it turned easily, too.

The stone wall began to **shake**. A slab of stone

moved aside with a **groan** to reveal a stone column with words carved into it:

Here lies the Lost Treasure of the Prehistoric Pirates: The Crystal Compass

A **mysterious** object rested on the top of the column. And on the stone wall behind the column, we saw more words engraved . . .

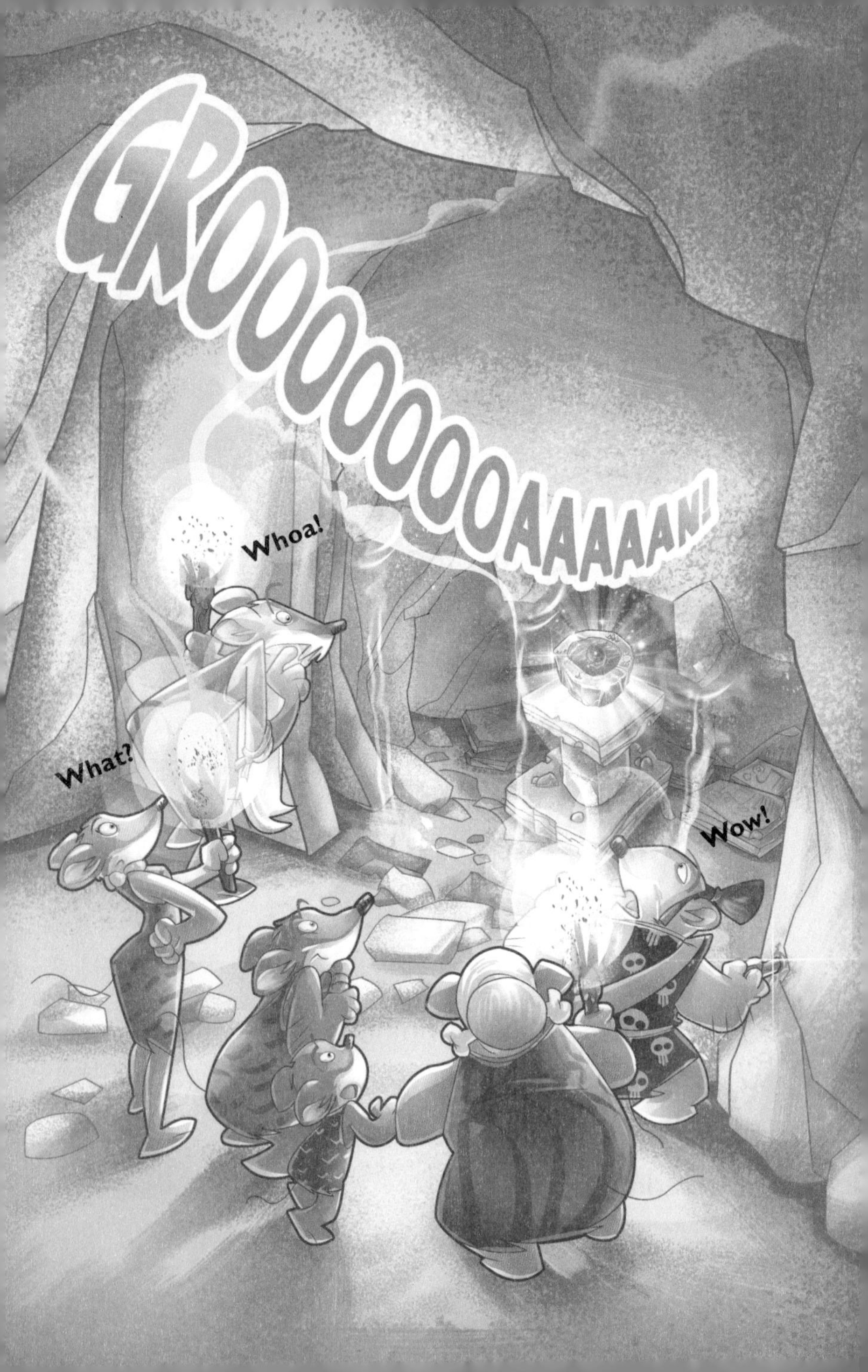
GROOOOOOOAAAAAN!
Whoa!
What?
Wow!

BEHOLD THE CRYSTAL COMPASS!
MORE VALUABLE THAN GOLD,
IT HAS TRAVELED THE GLOBE
WITH THE PIRATES OF OLD.
THE RODENT WHO HAS IT
MUST BE BRAVE AND BOLD
AND JOURNEY THE SEAS:
THERE ARE SIGHTS TO BEHOLD!
ADVENTURE AWAITS HIM,
AND TALES STILL UNTOLD!

Here lies the Lost
Treasure of the
Prehistoric Pirates:
The Crystal Compass

"I found it! I mean *we* found it!" Bart Barnacle cried out happily.

Then he scratched his head. "A CRYSTAL COMPASS? What kind of treasure is that?"

Thea pointed to more writing ETCHED into the wall. "Look, that explains it all."

Bart's eyes filled with tears as he read

COMPASS

A compass is an instrument that can help you find your way home. Its magnetic needle always points north — toward the Land of Ice. Once you figure out where north is, it will be easy to figure out the other directions: east (the Land of the Rising Sun and home to the prehistoric pirates), south (the Land of Fire), and west (the Land of the Setting Sun).

ICE   RISING SUN   FIRE   SETTING SUN

about the compass. "Friends, do you know what this means? Thanks to this treasure, I can **return** home! I can see Grandpa Blackbeard again, and all my friends and family!"

THERE IS NOTHING MORE PRECIOUS THAN HOME, THE PLACE WHERE WE FEEL THE MOST LOVED!

THE LAND OF ICE (NORTH)

THE LAND OF THE RISING SUN (EAST)

THE LAND OF THE SETTING SUN (WEST)

THE LAND OF FIRE (SOUTH)

MOUSENAPPED!

Now that we had found the Lost Treasure of the Prehistoric Pirates, we needed to get back to *Old Mouse City*. But to get back to Old Mouse City, we had to pass through the Hey Hey Forest again!

We did not want the musky baboons to **bombard** us with another coconut storm. Just the thought of running into that megalithic danger again made my whiskers tremble with fright.

"Well, at least the baboons are not as dangerous as the SABER-TOOTHED TIGERS," Benjamin reminded me.

So we set out into the forest, moving as

quietly as we could.

None of us made a single squeak as we walked through the woods. This time, the place seemed unusually quiet.

How strange . . .

There were no movements in the trees or coconuts flying at our heads. In fact, everything was very calm.

How very strange . . .

The baboons seemed to have vanished into thin air!

HOW VERY, VERY, VERY STRANGE . . .

But before we realized why things were actually so strange, a huge furry mass leaped down on us from above.

ROOOOOOOOAAAAAAR!

IT WAS A SABER-TOOTHED TIGER!

The **FEROCIOUS** feline had jumped down from a very tall palm tree and landed right in front of us.

"Primeval Parmesan!" Grandma Ratrock cried. "The musky baboons must have called in their allies, the saber-toothed tigers, to help them. Prepare to fight back!"

The **SCARY BEAST** jumped over us and grabbed the **chubbiest** one in our group — Bart Barnacle! Then the tiger swung away on a vine, mousenapping Bart and his treasure.

TRUMPETING TRICERATOPS, NOW WHAT?

FLUFFY, HELP US!

We knew we had to help Bart Barnacle **quickly** before the tigers gobbled him up. But nobody moved at first. We had no idea what to do. Thankfully, Grandma Ratrock started ordering us around.

"What are we doing here, standing around like *spineless* strings of **cheese**? Bart Barnacle has been mousenapped by a tiger! So we must hurry to the camp of the Saber-Toothed Squad in **Bugville**!"

The thought made my fur curl in fright. Bugville is the most **DANGEROUS, SCARY,** and **disgusting** place in the entire Stone Age!

"Be BRAVE!" Grandma shouted. "What are we waiting for? Let's race to **Bugville**!"

"And how are we supposed to free Bart Barnacle?" I asked. "We can't just MARCH IN and attack the tigers."

"Geronimo's right," Bluster agreed. "They'll put us in their Sunday soup and **chew** us up into tiny pieces!"

"But Bart Barnacle needs us," said Benjamin. "We can't just abandon him."

They'll chew us up!

"That's right!" Thea said.

Grandma Ratrock was deep in thought. I knew I shouldn't interrupt her or she might BONK me on the head.

Then her eyes brightened. "LISTEN

UP!" she called out. "I have an idea. To help Bart Barnacle, we need to go back to the Cave of Memories and ask for help from the only creature stronger than the saber-toothed tigers: Fluffy!"

"Yes!" Benjamin cried. "What's better than a **CAVE BEAR** to fight the tigers?"

So we quickly made our way back to the cave, where we once again found the rodent guardian and his **always-hungry** bear, Fluffy.

"Password!" the guardian commanded.

Silence, you fossilized fool!

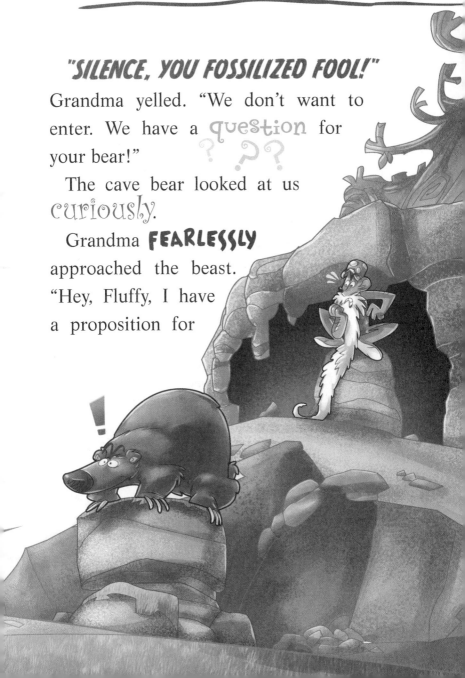

"SILENCE, YOU FOSSILIZED FOOL!"

Grandma yelled. "We don't want to enter. We have a question for your bear!"

The cave bear looked at us curiously.

Grandma **FEARLESSLY** approached the beast. "Hey, Fluffy, I have a proposition for you," she began. "And I know that you'll like it. You're a bear, right? And bears love **honey**. So listen closely, Fluffy. If you will help us save our friend from the saber-toothed tigers, I will make you a **MEGA-HONEY CAKE** stuffed with **honey**, covered with **HONEY GLAZE**, and decorated with **honey candy**. What do you say?"

Fluffy began to wag his stubby tail and drool.

"YUM, YUM, YUM!"

Grandma Ratrock shook paws with the bear. Fluffy was going to help!

Then Fluffy started to make gestures with his **PAWS**. Grandma understood. Fluffy had two **brothers** who could help, but they would each also need a mega-honey cake. So she would have to prepare **THREE** cakes in all.

"**IT'S A DEAL**, Fluffy," Grandma said. "Call your brothers."

ROOOAAAARR!

Fluffy stood up on his hind legs and took in a huge **MOUTHFUL** of air. His chest **puffed** up so big that he looked twice his size! Then he cupped his front paws around his mouth and let out a **TERRIFYING** roar that shook the entire prehistoric forest.

ROOOAAAARRR!

Seconds later, two big, scary-looking **CAVE BEARS** ran right up to Fluffy.

YIKES! Instead of just one bear, now we had **THREE HUNGRY BEARS** in front of us!

I began to shake like a prehistoric cheese custard. Bluster, Thea, and Benjamin didn't look so **calm**, either.

Grandma Ratrock wasn't scared at all. She smiled at Fluffy and **patted** him on the head.

"Well done, Fluffy," she said. "Now the family is **complete**!"

Fluffy grunted to his brothers to explain Grandma's proposal, and the other two bears licked their WHiSKeRS.

Then Grandma Ratrock jumped on Fluffy's back.

Well done!

"What are you **lazybones** all waiting for?" she asked. "Jump on a bear and follow us!"

Then Fluffy galloped off at the speed of a **tornado** while Grandma tightly gripped his fur.

Grandma's bravery gave us all COURAGE. Thea and Bluster jumped on one bear, and I jumped on the other with

Benjamin. Then we *RACED* toward Bugville — five cavemice and three cave bears going to attack the Saber-Toothed Squad.

What a fabumouse adventure!

BEARS VS. TIGERS!

Despite their size, the bears were **FAST** and ran like the wind. We quickly **ZIGZAGGED** between buzzing

flies, bothersome mosquitoes, and stinky puddles.

We had arrived in **Bugville**! A horrible **stench** hit our snouts. The nasty smell even made our eyes water.

"The tiger camp must be nearby!" Grandma called out.

We traveled through the SWAMPY lands of Bugville until we found the camp of the SABER-TOOTHED SQUAD. Just seeing the tigers' huts sent a chill through my fur. But there was no time to be afraid!

"ATTACK!" Grandma Ratrock urged the cave bears.

The speed and power of the bears caught the tigers completely by surprise. They began to run away, meowing like scaredy-cats and bumping into one another.

SMASH! The bears started to jump onto the straw huts of the tigers, crushing them with their weight.

Then Tiger Khan, the leader of the felines, began to YELL at his troops.

"Stop running away! Fight back!" he SHOUTED.

But the tigers were too frightened —

and the bears were just too **POWERFUL** to stop. They stomped their way through the camp, destroying everything in their path.

Listen up! Stop running! Move it! Fight back!

"TAKE THAT, TIGERS!" Grandma Ratrock taunted them. "Better stay away from me! I'll wipe those **SILLY STRIPES** right off your fur!"

"That will teach you to mousenap our friends, you *STINKY* cats!" Thea yelled.

That reminded me.

WHERE WAS BART BARNACLE?

I looked around. The fleeing tigers were kicking up dirt as they ran. When the dust cleared, I saw Bart TIED UP and hanging like a cheese in a shop window.

"Let's go, Uncle Ger!" Benjamin yelled. "We have to help him!"

He steered our bear toward the pirate. The cave bear cut the ropes with his **SHARP TEETH**, and Bart slid onto the bear's back.

Over here!

"Bart Barnacle is free!"

I cried out happily.

Then we all raced away from Bugville as fast as our bears would take us. We left the saber-toothed tigers to lick their **WOUNDS** in their ruined camp.

MISSION ACCOMPLISHED!

YUM, YUM, YUM!

When we came back to Old Mouse City riding those three **GIANT CAVE BEARS**, our fellow cavemice screamed in fright! They thought they were about to become extinct.

Ernest Heftymouse, the village chief, slowly approached us with trembling whiskers.

"St-Stiltonoot, wh-what happened?" he stammered. "Why have you returned with these th-three ferocious cave bears?"

Grandma Ratrock and Fluffy moved closer to him. *"PIPE DOWN, HEFTYMOUSE!"* she said crossly.

Everyone quieted down. "These bears were once our **enemies**, but they are now friends of our village," she announced. "Without them, we would never have returned to *Old Mouse City*. So don't mess with them!"

Ernest eyed them **suspiciously**, but the bears responded with dazzling smiles, showing off all their sharp teeth.

Then Bluster told the tale of our incredible ADVENTURE with the three cave bears, and Ernest calmed down.

The three bears turned to Grandma. Then they pointed to their mouths and grunted.

"YUM, YUM, YUM?"

Grandma smiled. "Of course! I didn't forget my promise," she said. "Let me go prepare three MEGA-HONEY CAKES for you. I will use the finest honey in the village!"

It took Grandma a whole day and a whole night to make them, but in the end, the three enormouse honey cakes were finished. They were so big that Grandma had to use a PUSHCART to wheel them to the town square, where the bear brothers were waiting.

My cousin Trap tried to steal a **BITE** because he loves honey. (What food doesn't he love?) But Grandma waved her **CLUB** at him.

"Stop that, Grandson!" she scolded. "You didn't do anything to help us, so you don't get any cake!"

As the **THREE BEARS** began to devour the honey cakes, the citizens of our village arrived carrying platters of other **delicious** foods. Everything was honey flavored in honor of our new honey-loving friends!

Ernest Heftymouse cleared his throat. "This is just a small gesture of **thanks** to our new bear friends," he announced. "If you ever want to come back to help us defend against the **SABER-TOOTHED TIGERS** again, we will be grateful."

The bears smiled and looked over the food:

- a mound of honey-covered **GREEN CHEESE**

- a **Jurassic cheesecake** with honey drizzle
- a **pickled pterodactyl egg** with creamed honey
- a mound of **BONE SHANKS** with honey sauce

Wow! Our friends **gobbled** up everything in a flash. When they were finished stuffing themselves, they got ready to leave.

"**Thank you** again for saving our friend Bart from the tigers," I told them.

Trap **elbowed** me. "Hey, Cousin, you still haven't explained the most important thing. What is the Lost Treasure of the Prehistoric Pirates? Tell me what it is! I'm so curious!"

All the residents of Old Mouse City PIPED UP.

"Yes, tell us, Stiltonoot!"

HIP, HIP, HOORAY!

Bart Barnacle showed everyone the CRYSTAL COMPASS that we had found.

Trap eyed it **greedily**. "Nice, but how much is it worth? Can we sell it and become RICH?"

Grandma Ratrock shook her head. "Grandson, you don't understand one bit! This compass is not precious because it is worth a lot of **shells**. It's precious because it will allow our friend to return home! AND THAT IS THE BEST TREASURE OF ALL!"

She continued scolding Trap. "Have you learned a lesson here, or do I need to **BONK** you on the head with my club to make my point?"

"No, no, I get it!" Trap said.

"Good!" said Grandma. "And now you will organize a **huge banquet** for the village so that we can celebrate!"

Thea smiled. "Great idea! A party is just what we need!"

Trap and Greasella Stonyfur worked all day long to cook up enough food for a banquet. As the sun set, I headed toward the port with Bart Barnacle and the other citizens of Old Mouse City, laughing and joking.

When we arrived at the Rotten Tooth Tavern, we couldn't believe all the food that Trap and Greasella had prepared. There was

cheese pie, and **cheese** balls, and cheese bread, and **cheese** stew . . . it was a **fabumouse feast**!

It was a great way to celebrate finding the Lost Treasure of the Prehistoric Pirates. But then things got even better!

I was about to dig in when the smell of lily-scented perfume wafted by my whiskers.

"Geronimo!" called out a sweet, lovely voice.

I turned and found myself snout-to-snout with the most **fascinating**, interesting,

107

and **intelligent** mouse in all of prehistory. The nicest, most beautiful rodent: Clarissa Conjurat.

Clarissa took my paw and squeezed it. (And she really squeezed it hard. Besides being intelligent and beautiful, she is also **SUPER-STRONG**!)

"Thank you so much for bringing my father back safe and sound," she said with a smile that **MELTED** my heart like cheese fondue.

I was so nervous around her that I was shaking like cheese-flavored jelly!

"Um, clanks, Tharissa," I said. "I mean, thanks,

Thank you, Geronimo!

Clarissa. I just did my worst. I mean, my best. Squeak!"

Luckily, I was interrupted by Bart Barnacle, who wanted to thank us all.

"Dear cavemice," he began. "This adventure has made me realize one **VERY IMPORTANT THING**. I thought I had lost my friends. But I found new ones! I will never forget you."

"We won't forget you, Bart Barnacle!" everyone cheered.

Grandma Ratrock cheered the loudest.

"HOORAY FOR BART! HIP, HIP, HOORAY!"

We all echoed Grandma Ratrock. **"HOORAY!"**

When the celebration ended, I returned
to my cave to enjoy a well-deserved rest. I
had a hard day of work to look forward to
when I woke up: chiseling a special edition
of *The Stone Gazette*. It would be all about
our sensational discoveries in the
Cave of Memories!

It had truly been an exciting adventure.
But I knew that an even more exciting
adventure was just around the corner . . . or
I'm not

Geronimo Stiltonoot,
cavemouse!

Don't miss any adventures of the cavemice!

#1 The Stone of Fire

#2 Watch Your Tail!

#3 Help, I'm in Hot Lava!

#4 The Fast and the Frozen

#5 The Great Mouse Race

#6 Don't Wake the Dinosaur!

#7 I'm a Scaredy-Mouse!

#8 Surfing for Secrets

#9 Get the Scoop, Geronimo!

Be sure to read all my fabumouse adventures!

#1 Lost Treasure of the Emerald Eye

#2 The Curse of the Cheese Pyramid

#3 Cat and Mouse in a Haunted House

#4 I'm Too Fond of My Fur!

#5 Four Mice Deep in the Jungle

#6 Paws Off, Cheddarface!

#7 Red Pizzas for a Blue Count

#8 Attack of the Bandit Cats

#9 A Fabumouse Vacation for Geronimo

#10 All Because of a Cup of Coffee

#11 It's Halloween, You 'Fraidy Mouse!

#12 Merry Christmas, Geronimo!

#13 The Phantom of the Subway

#14 The Temple of the Ruby of Fire

#15 The Mona Mousa Code

#16 A Cheese-Colored Camper

#17 Watch Your Whiskers, Stilton!

#18 Shipwreck on the Pirate Islands

#19 My Name Is Stilton, Geronimo Stilton

#20 Surf's Up, Geronimo!

| #21 The Wild, Wild West | #22 The Secret of Cacklefur Castle | A Christmas Tale | #23 Valentine's Day Disaster | #24 Field Trip to Niagara Falls |

| #25 The Search for Sunken Treasure | #26 The Mummy with No Name | #27 The Christmas Toy Factory | #28 Wedding Crasher | #29 Down and Out Down Under |

| #30 The Mouse Island Marathon | #31 The Mysterious Cheese Thief | Christmas Catastrophe | #32 Valley of the Giant Skeletons | #33 Geronimo and the Gold Medal Mystery |

| #34 Geronimo Stilton, Secret Agent | #35 A Very Merry Christmas | #36 Geronimo's Valentine | #37 The Race Across America | #38 A Fabumouse School Adventure |

| #39 Singing Sensation | #40 The Karate Mouse | #41 Mighty Mount Kilimanjaro | #42 The Peculiar Pumpkin Thief | #43 I'm Not a Supermouse! |

#44 The Giant
Diamond Robbery

#45 Save the White
Whale!

#46 The Haunted
Castle

#47 Run for the Hills,
Geronimo!

#48 The Mystery in
Venice

#49 The Way of
the Samurai

#50 This Hotel Is
Haunted!

#51 The Enormouse
Pearl Heist

#52 Mouse in Space!

#53 Rumble in
the Jungle

#54 Get into Gear,
Stilton!

#55 The Golden
Statue Plot

#56 Flight of the
Red Bandit

Special Edition!
The Hunt for the
Golden Book

#57 The Stinky
Cheese Vacation

#58 The Super
Chef Contest

#59 Welcome to
Moldy Manor

Special Edition!
The Hunt for the
Curious Cheese

#60 The Treasure of
Easter Island

#61 Mouse House
Hunter

*Don't miss
my journeys
through time!*

MEET GERONIMO STILTONIX

He is a spacemouse — the Geronimo Stilton of a parallel universe! He is captain of the spaceship *MouseStar 1*. While flying through the cosmos, he visits distant planets and meets crazy aliens. His adventures are out of this world!

#1 Alien Escape

#2 You're Mine, Captain!

#3 Ice Planet Adventure

#4 The Galactic Goal

#5 Rescue Rebellion

Don't miss these exciting Thea Sisters adventures!

Thea Stilton and the Dragon's Code

Thea Stilton and the Mountain of Fire

Thea Stilton and the Ghost of the Shipwreck

Thea Stilton and the Secret City

Thea Stilton and the Mystery in Paris

Thea Stilton and the Cherry Blossom Adventure

Thea Stilton and the Star Castaways

Thea Stilton: Big Trouble in the Big Apple

Thea Stilton and the Ice Treasure

Thea Stilton and the Secret of the Old Castle

Thea Stilton and the Blue Scarab Hunt

Thea Stilton and the Prince's Emerald

Thea Stilton and the Mystery on the Orient Express

Thea Stilton and the Dancing Shadows

Thea Stilton and the Legend of the Fire Flowers

Thea Stilton and the Spanish Dance Mission

Thea Stilton and the Journey to the Lion's Den

Thea Stilton and the Great Tulip Heist

Thea Stilton and the Chocolate Sabotage

Thea Stilton and the Missing Myth

Thea Stilton and the Lost Letters

Meet
CREEPELLA VON CACKLEFUR

I, *Geronimo Stilton*, have a lot of mouse friends, but none as **spooky** as my friend CREEPELLA VON CACKLEFUR! She is an enchanting and MYSTERIOUS mouse with a pet bat named **Bitewing**. YIKES! I'm a real 'fraidy mouse, but even I think CREEPELLA and her family are AWFULLY fascinating. I can't wait for you to read all about CREEPELLA in these a-mouse-ly funny and **spectacularly spooky** tales!

#1 The Thirteen Ghosts

#2 Meet Me in Horrorwood

#3 Ghost Pirate Treasure

#4 Return of the Vampire

#5 Fright Night

#6 Ride for Your Life!

#7 A Suitcase Full of Ghosts

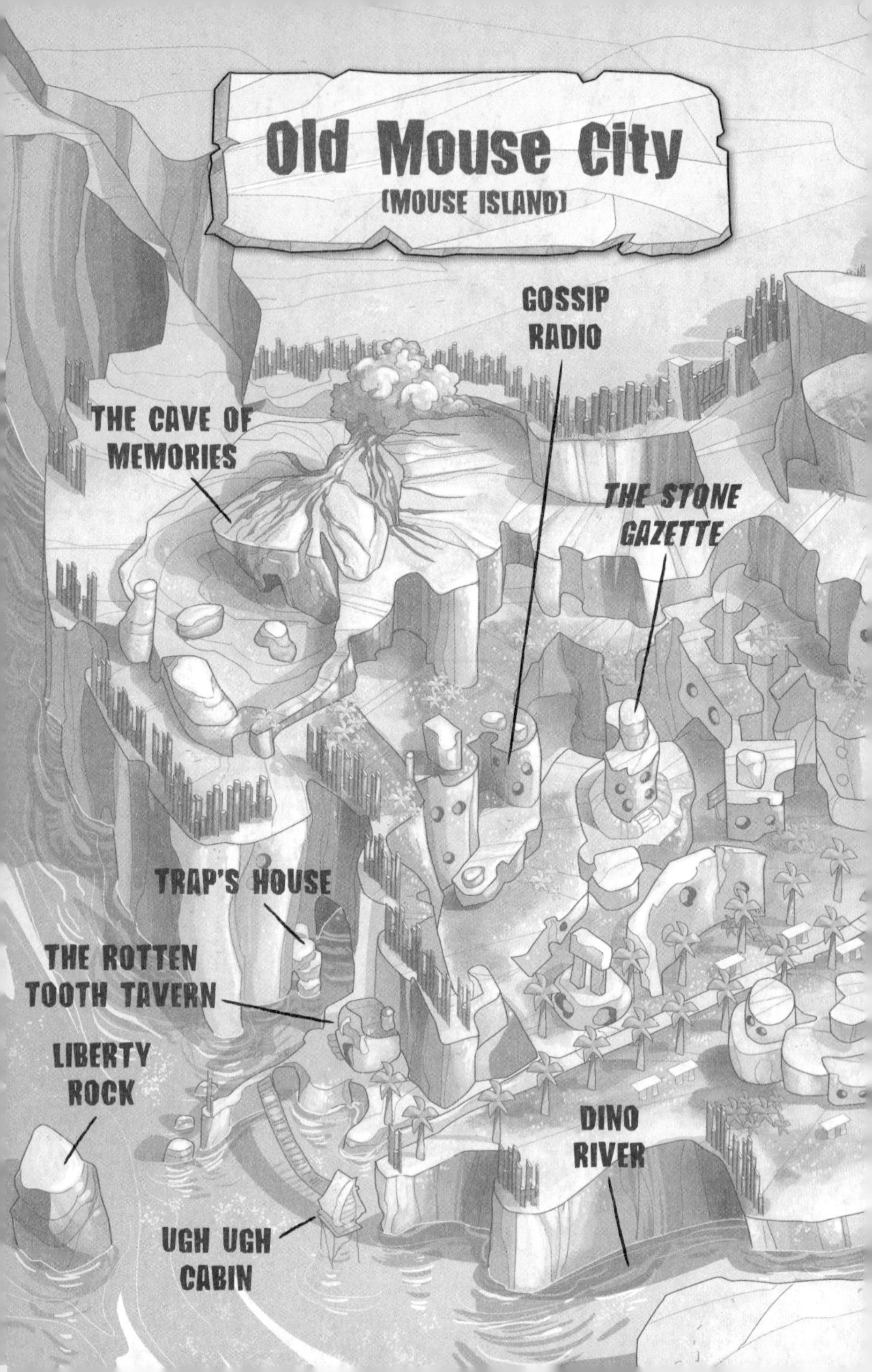

Old Mouse City
(MOUSE ISLAND)

GOSSIP RADIO

THE CAVE OF MEMORIES

THE STONE GAZETTE

TRAP'S HOUSE

THE ROTTEN TOOTH TAVERN

LIBERTY ROCK

UGH UGH CABIN

DINO RIVER

DEAR MOUSE FRIENDS,

THANKS FOR READING,

AND GOOD-BYE UNTIL

THE NEXT BOOK!